TWO WAYS HOME

A FOSTER CARE JOURNEY

BY
MARION RHINES

ILLUSTRATED BY
REBEKAH WOOD

*Nancy-
Thanks for all
you do!
Marion
Rhines*

TWO WAYS HOME: A FOSTER CARE JOURNEY

1405 SW 6th Avenue • Ocala, Florida 34471 • Phone 352-622-1825 • Fax 352-622-1875
Website: www.atlantic-pub.com • Email: sales@atlantic-pub.com
SAN Number: 268-1250

Library of Congress Cataloging-in-Publication Data

Names: Rhines, Marion, author. Title: Two ways home : a foster care journey / by: Marion Rhines.
Description: Ocala, Florida : Atlantic Publishing Group, Inc., [2019]
Summary: Ten-year-old Eli explains why he is in foster care, describes his foster family and team of caregivers, and ponders the good and unexpected things that can happen while in foster care.
Identifiers: LCCN 2019011293 (print) | LCCN 2019015922 (ebook) | ISBN 9781620236420 (ebook) | ISBN 9781620236413 (pbk.) | ISBN 1620236419 (pbk.)
Subjects: | CYAC: Foster children—Fiction. | Foster home care—Fiction. | Family life—Fiction.
Classification: LCC PZ7.1.R4935 (ebook) | LCC PZ7.1.R4935 Tw 2019 (print) | DDC [E]—dc23 LC record available at https://lccn.loc.gov/2019011293

Printed in the United States .

PROJECT MANAGER: Katie Cline
INTERIOR LAYOUT: Nicole Sturk

FOREWORD

My children may not look like me, they may not have my nose, my eyes, or my smile, but the resemblance is there, you just may not see it. *They have my heart.*

–KATHY L. H. MENDOZA

Foster and adoptive parents recognize the truth in these words.

Another truth about fostering and adopting is that the children who join our families don't care how much we know until they know how much we care. This book, written by a seasoned foster and adoptive mother, is one example of going the extra mile to help children better understand the foster care system and just what it means to join another family until they can rejoin their original family or join a family through adoption.

Foster and adoptive parents are ordinary people who do extraordinary things. Please consider how you can be a part of these most rewarding experiences as you read this book and learn more about bringing children into your family.

IRENE CLEMENTS, NFPA, Executive Director

Hi, my name is Levi. I'm 10 years old! I live with a foster family because I can't live with my own family right now, but that's okay. This is Benny. He's 5. He can't live with his family, either. I have lived with a foster family once before, but this is Benny's first time. Our foster parents are Keith and Liz, but Benny calls them mom and dad, and that's okay too!

When I found out I was coming to another foster home, I was nervous. But once I got here, my scared feeling went away. It was summertime, so we stayed up late and watched one of my favorite movies. Living with a foster family sometimes feels like being on a long sleepover weekend. This family already had four children at the house: Julian, Marie, Henry, and Tomás. They also have a dog named Max. And now, there's me and Benny, so things can get pretty crazy around here!

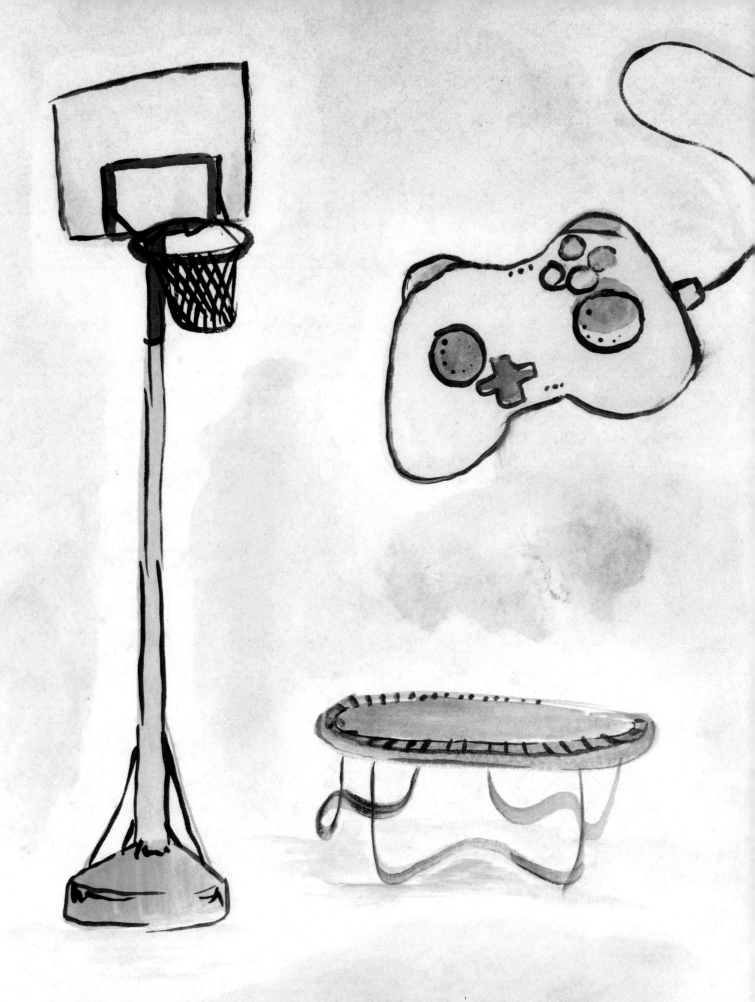

Having so many children in the house can be fun and noisy. There is always something going on. Julian is 18 and likes to play video games when he isn't studying for college or working. Marie is 11 and sometimes plays school with all of us. She is the teacher. Henry, Benny, and I like to jump on the trampoline, shoot basketball, play with action figures, and play video games. Tomás also likes to play video games and make up interesting characters! Sometimes, it gets too loud, and Tomás puts on his headphones. Loud noises scare him.

I share a room with Henry. He's 13. Henry was a foster child like me and was adopted by Keith and Liz when he was 9. We have bunk beds and take turns sleeping on the top bunk! Benny shares a room with Tomás, who is 4 years old. Tomás was adopted by Keith and Liz as a baby. He has family from Guatemala. In our rooms, Benny and I have space for our toys, clothes, and pictures of our families. I have a picture of my mom and stepdad right where I can see it.

Being in foster care means that Benny and I have lots of people to help look after us. Ana, my caseworker, checks on me and makes sure I have everything I need. My foster parents go to meetings with Ana where they decide what has to happen before I can go back to my parents. Benny has a caseworker named Renee. I also go to the doctor and dentist to stay healthy. When I want to talk about things, I can go see my therapist, John. Talking makes me feel so much better! Nurse Kellie makes sure my medicine is working and that I feel good. I love Kellie! And Keith and Liz help us too! Every month they take Benny and me to visit our moms, and Liz helps us talk to our moms on the phone.

School can be a bit different when you live with a foster family. If you have to change schools when you go to a different family, it can be hard because you miss your old friends and teachers. But when I got to my new school, I recognized a teacher from my old school. I started on the first day already knowing somebody! Keith and Liz try really hard to participate in my school life. They volunteer in my class and sometimes go on school trips. I can always ask them to help me with homework. They even helped Benny make a costume for Career Day.

I feel kind of sad not being with my mom and stepdad every day, but I can always find someone to do stuff with. My foster dad's family lives here in town, and I get to see Nana and Papa, Uncle Kevin, Aunt Karen, and Cousin Tim all the time. Holidays are lots of fun because we all get together at our house. After dinner on Thanksgiving, we all made Christmas crafts together. Benny and I made ornaments with our pictures on them to hang on the tree with the rest of the family.

Keith and Liz have been foster parents to a bunch of children. Our walls at home are filled with their photos. First, there was Tina. She was a senior in high school. Then Henry came to live here before Tina left. Then Tomás came a little bit before Jenny. She was 5 years old and from a country in Africa! She got to go home. It is neat to see the photos of the other children who have been here.

Sometimes good things happen unexpectedly in foster care. I found out today that Benny will be going home soon! It will be strange when he leaves, but I'm glad he gets to go home. Ana told me recently that I won't be able to go back home, but that I'm getting adopted. I was really sad at first, but I like to watch wrestling, so Liz explained it to me like this. My foster parents and my parents are like wrestling teammates. My mom and stepdad have done the best they can, but now they need to "tap out" and let my foster parents have a turn taking care of me. Keith and Liz love me so much that they want me to stay and be their son!

It takes a lot of people working together to take care of foster kids like me. My new family might not be as traditional as some others, but I love it! I guess it doesn't matter how different your family is as long as you're loved and cared for. You might say there are two ways home!

ABOUT THE AUTHOR

Marion Rhines has been a contributing writer to the Fostering Families Today magazine, drawing from her experience as a foster/adoptive parent. She lives with her family in Knoxville, Tennessee. She is the wife of a military veteran, mother of five children, and has also been a private child-care provider, substitute teacher, and a medical office receptionist. She gets her best ideas from her real life. Marion loves to write poems, many of which have been turned into bookmarks for foster parents and the lyrics to a song.

ABOUT THE ILLUSTRATOR

Rebekah Wood is a high school senior in Rock Hill, South Carolina. This is her first children's book, and she looks forward to illustrating many more. She spends her time leading the school's Art Club and painting murals across campus. She is currently working on her AP Portfolio in Art, which is based on her experience with chronic pain and NDPH. Even in pain, she loves to create artwork with oil pastels, watercolor, charcoal, and acrylic. She will attend Winthrop University in the fall and will work toward a degree in art. Rebekah plans to paint worlds and feelings for the rest of her life.

AFTER THE STORY

1. How did Levi feel about being in foster care at the beginning of the book? How did he feel at the end of the book?

2. In what ways did Keith and Liz show how important their roles as foster parents were to them? What things did they do to show support to Levi and Benny's birth families?

3. What were some things Levi did to help overcome his feelings of sadness when he missed his birth family?

4. How did Levi and Benny get along with the other children in the family?

5. What was Levi's reaction to Benny going back home to his birth family?

6. What was Levi's reaction to being adopted by Keith and Liz?

7. What are some ways that love was shown throughout the book?

JUV013090 JUVENILE FICTION / Family / Alternative Family
JUV013050 JUVENILE FICTION / Family / Orphans & Foster Homes
JUV039090 JUVENILE FICTION / Social Themes / New Experience

$19.95

L357

10-YEAR-OLD LEVI HAS JUST JOINED A NEW FOSTER FAMILY!

Levi knows living with a new family can be daunting, but wants everyone know about all the good things that can come from foster care. With vibrant watercolor illustrations and a kid-friendly story, "Two Ways Home: A Foster Care Journey" can help children learn more about their new situation and feel more comfortable with their foster family!

Atlantic Publishing Group, Inc.

Your complete resource for small business, management, finance, online, real estate, and young adult books covering subjects such as careers, college life, education, finance, history, lifestyle, and writing.
We have a book for that.™

1405 SW 6th Ave • Ocala, FL 34471-0640
Phone 352-622-1825 • Fax 352-622-1875
www.atlantic-pub.com

ISBN-13: 97816202

51995

9 781620 236413

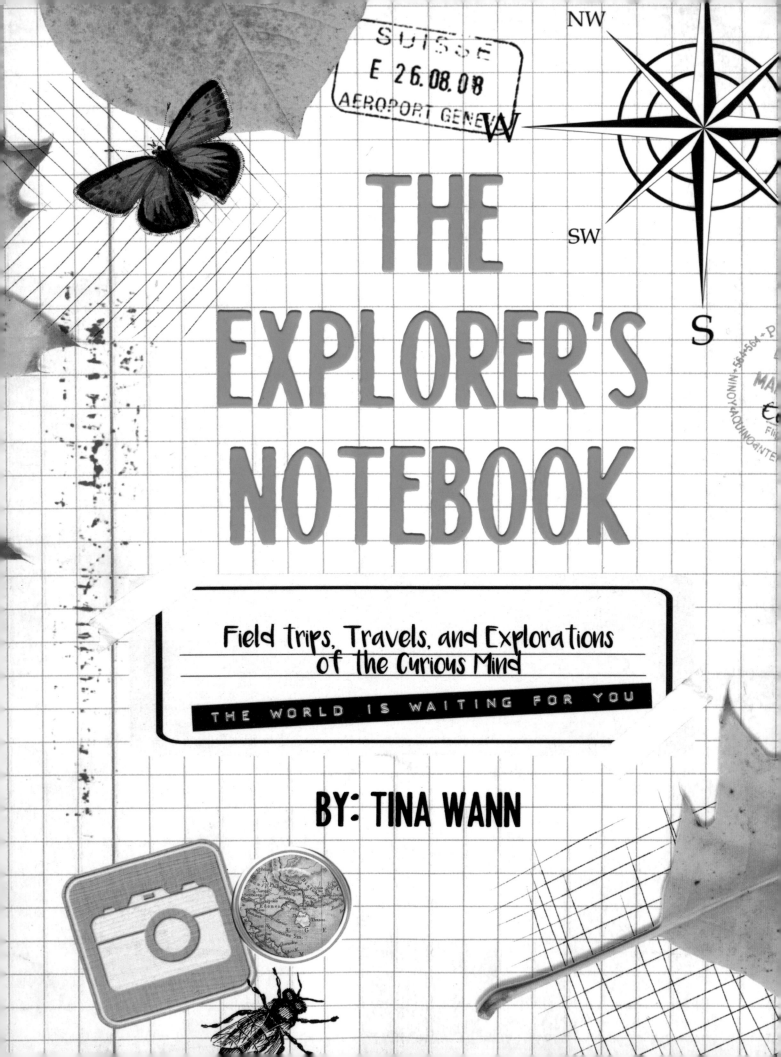

THE EXPLORER'S NOTEBOOK

Field trips, Travels, and Explorations
of the Curious Mind

THE WORLD IS WAITING FOR YOU

BY: TINA WANN